D1539648

TICKET TO
DREAMLAND

_____

Passenger's Name

There's a Train Out for DREAMLAND

By Frederich H. Heider & Carl Kress

Illustrated by Jane Dyer & Brooke Dyer

HARPER

An Imprint of HarperCollinsPublishers

Library of Congress Cataloging-in-Publication Data

Heider, Frederich H.

There's a train out for dreamland / by Frederich H. Heider & Carl Kress ; illustrated by Jane Dyer & Brooke Dyer. — 1st ed.

p.   cm.

Summary: As a train heads out to dreamland, it travels on peppermint rails through a confectionary landscape.

ISBN 978-0-06-058021-6 (trade bdg.) — ISBN 978-0-06-058022-3 (lib. bdg.)

1. Children's songs, English—United States—Texts. [1. Songs. 2. Railroad trains—Songs and music. 3. Candy—Songs and

music.] I. Kress, Carl, 1907–1965. II. Dyer, Jane, ill. III. Dyer, Brooke, ill. IV. Title. V. Title: There is a train out for dreamland.

PZ8.3.H4128Th 2010   2009030934   782.42—dc22   CIP   [E]   AC

Typography by Rachel Zegar

10 11 12 13 14   SCP   10 9 8 7 6 5 4 3 2 1

❖

First Edition

To Blue
—J.D. & B.D.

DING, DONG, DING, DONG,

Hear a bell a-ringing.

All the children singing.

You'll be singing too.

Whoo-oo, whoo-oo,

Hear a whistle blowing.
Soon they'll all be going.
You'll be going too.

There's a train
out for
DREAMLAND
that rides on a

peppermint rail.

It only stops at ice-cream stations
To pick up crackerjack mail.

There's a train
out for
DREAMLAND.
It's run by a chocolate

brown bear.

It puffs around a candy mountain

As it sails through the air.

You'll see a big white snowman
Who melts when he hears you laugh.
A singing mouse,

A licorice house,

And a funny-looking jelly bean giraffe.

We'll *CHOO-CHOO, CHOO-CHOO*

to the skies.

So, if you want

to go to

DREAMLAND,

Well, then just close your eyes.

There's a Train Out for Dreamland
By Frederich H. Heider & Carl Kress